KINGS & KINGDOMS 1

Y AKHILESH

NOTE: ALL THE PICTURES SHOWN IN THIS BOOK ARE NOT REAL AND THE CREDITS FOR THOSE PICTURES GO TO UNSPLASH.COM WHERE YOU GET FREE IMAGES. THANK YOU UNSPLASH

Contents

CHAPTER I

Introduction

INDEX

NOTE: ALL THE PICTURES SHOWN IN THIS BOOK ARE NOT REAL AND THE CREDITS FOR THOSE PICTURES GO TO UNSPLASH.COM WHERE YOU GET FREE IMAGES. THANK YOU UNSPLASH AND PLEASE FORGIVE ME IF THERE ARE ANY SPELLING MISTAKES.

INTRO: IN THE YEAR 1669 A KING NAMED WILLIAM WITH HIS WIFE LIVED IN A KINGDOM. THEY HAVE 3 SONS ELDER ONE NAME IS APEX, THE MIDDLE ONE NAME IS DANE AND THE YOUNGER ONE NAME IS MICHAEL. THERE WAS A BIG KINGDOM RIGHT IN BETWEEN ALL OTHER KINGDOMS WHICH EVERY KING WANTS TO RULE BUT THE KING WHO IS RULING THAT KINGDOM WAS GEORGE. HE HAS OVER A 1.2LAKH ARMY WITH 20,000 ELEPHANTS AND 70,000 HORSES. THE ONLY THING WHICH MAKES

GEORGE POWERFUL IS HIS KINGDOM "MIDLAND" CAUSE EVERYONE WHO RULES THIS KINGDOM CAN HAVE A GIANT ARMY WITH ELEPHANTS AND HORSES. THIS STORY IS ABOUT HOW WILLIAM AND HIS SONS WILL TAKE MIDLAND BY RULING A SMALL KINGDOM "WEST SIGHT" AND RULE IT.

CHARACTER : WILLIAM,LILITH,APEX,DANE,MICHAEL AND FEW SIDE CHARACTERS

SUMMARY: ONE FINE DAY EMPEROR WILLIAM ORDERS APEX TO GO TO THE OCEAN SIDE AND SEE THE CRIMES CAUSED BY PIRATES WITH A DECENT CREW. APEX WITHOUT SAYING ANYTHING GOES TO THE OCEAN WITH HIS 21 MEMBERS CREW IN A SHIP CALLED "BROWN WOOD". APEX WITH THE WORLD'S FASTEST SHIP WAS GOING TOWARDS THE OCEAN TO HELP PEOPLE WHO ARE VICTIMS OF PIRATE CRIMES. THEY ALL ARE WAITING FOR A DECADE TO CATCH THIS ONE PIRATE. AT THE FIRST IT WAS AN ORDER FOR APEX BUT AFTER THAT CATCHING THIS PIRATE IS A TASK FOR APEX AND APEX TOOK THIS AS A CHALLENGE. APEX AND HIS CREW REACHED THEIR PLACE. THEY STARTED INVESTIGATING PEOPLE ABOUT PIRATES AND THEY ASKED

FOR THE PIRATE "CAPTAIN MORNINGSTAR" BUT CAPT. MORNINGSTAR IS SO CLEVER THAT HE NEVER STEPS OUT OF HIS SHIP HE JUST TELLS THE PLAN AND THE WHOLE THING WORKS

OUT PERFECTLY.AFTER A FEW HOURS..... AS ALWAYS APEX DIDN'T FIND ANYTHING ABOUT PIRATES SO HE DECIDED TO GO BACK ON HIS SHIP. HE CALLED ALL HIS MEMBERS AND WENT TO HIS SHIP. AFTER A FEW DAYS OF SAILING AT NIGHT A BIG

STORM APPROACHES SO THEY NEED TO STOP THEIR SHIP. APEX STOPPED HIS BROWN WOODS NEAR A ISLAND AND ALL THE MEMBERS STARTED TO FIND A CAVE. ONE OF THEM WAS SUCCESSFUL IN THEIR JOB. ALL PEOPLE LIVED IN THAT CAVE. AFTER THE STORM COOLED THEY ALL WENT OUT AND SAILED AWAY FROM THAT ISLAND BUT WHILE GOING THEY NOTICED THAT THERE IS NO FUEL

BUT THEY WERE LUCKY ENOUGH THAT A SHIP APPROACHED IN DISTANCE SO THEY ASKED FOR THAT SHIP HELP AND THEY ACCEPTED. BROWN WOODS WAS TIED TO THE ANOTHER SHIP

AND WAS TAKEN TO A ISLAND NEARBY TO TIE IT UP. THEY TIED IT UP AND CAME BACK ON THIS SHIP. THE REASON WHY THEY TIED THAT SHIP IS THE CAPTAIN OF THIS SHIP TOLD WE CAN'T TAKE THAT BROWN WOODS WITH HIS NORMAL SHIP SO HE GAVE A PLAN TO TIE IT UP ON AN ISLAND NEARBY. AT NIGHT APEX AND HIS CREW WERE APPROACHING WEST SIGHT SO APEX WENT TO THE SHIP CAPTAIN AND SAID THANK YOU AND ALSO SAID THAT HE WILL GIVE HIM A SHIP BUT THAT CAPTAIN TOLD "NO APEX, YOU ALREADY GAVE ME THE WORLDS FASTEST SHIP I DON'T NEED THAT ANYMORE" APEX WAS SHOCKED AND CAUGHT CAPTAIN'S COLLAR AND ASKED WHO ARE YOU?? "I AM CAPTAIN MORNINGSTAR," TOLD THE CAPTAIN. HE ALSO TOLD HIM THAT HE WAS ONLY THE PERSON TO TAKE ALL HIS FUEL OUT AND ALSO WANTEDLY GAVE HIM THE IDEA OF TYING THAT SHIP. CAPT. MORNINGSTAR THREW APEX AND HIS CREW INTO THE OCEAN WITHOUT A SMALL BOAT. APEX AND HIS CREW WERE SAILING IN THE WATER WITH NO HELP, BUT

THEN A BIG BOAT APPROACHED AND TO HIS SURPRISE IT WAS PRINCE DANE AND MICHAEL BOAT. APEX WAS HAPPY THAT HIS 2 BROTHERS HELPED HIM, BUT HE WAS ANGRY WITH MORNINGSTAR TOO...APEX EXPLAINED EVERYTHING TO DANE AND MICHAEL AND NOW THE THREE BROTHERS DECIDED TO CATCH CAPTAIN MORNINGSTAR. DANE SAID, "CATCHING MORNINGSTAR IS NOT EASY, WE NEED TO SPLIT INTO 3 DIRECTIONS WE HAVE NEARLY 42 MEMBERS EACH ONE WILL TAKE 14 MEMBERS WITH HIM." OKAY SAID MICHAEL AND APEX. NOW DANE WENT TO SOUTH, APEX TO EAST, AND MICHAEL TO NORTH AND THESE 3 BROTHERS ARE FROM WEST SO THEY DON'T NEED TO CHECK WEST. NORTH WAS OCEAN SO MICHAEL NEED TO GO TO IN A SHIP, BUT BECAUSE OF HIS FEAR OF THE OCEAN, HE TELLS APEX TO GO INSTEAD OF HIM AND APEX ACCEPTS IT. APEX WENT ON A NICE ARMORED SHIP AND NOW HE IS WAITING TO ENCOUNTER MORNINGSTAR ONCE AGAIN. MORNINGSTAR HERE IS CHILLING WITHOUT ANY FEAR. AT NIGHT A MAN WAS SWIMMING IN THE OCEAN. ACTUALLY, HE WAS DROWNING AND HE WAS SAVED BY APEX. APEX ASKED WHO ARE YOU? THEN THE MAN TOLD THAT HE IS A MIKE CREWMATE OF HENRY BINKS AND HE WAS BANISHED FROM THE SHIP FOR BEING WEAK TO DO WORK. APEX GOT AN IDEA, HE THOUGHT TO TAKE THE HELP OF HENRY TO CATCH MORNINGSTAR AND AFTER THAT CATCH HENRY TOO... SO HE ASKED MIKE ABOUT HENRY AND THEN HE TOLD THAT HENRY WENT IN SEARCH OF MORNINGSTAR. HE IS ANGRY WITH HIM AND HE WENT TOWARD THE SOUTH. NOW APEX FELT HAPPY CAUSE HE CAN TAKE HELP OF DANE IN THE

SOUTH.SO APEX TURNED HIS BOAT TOWARDS THE SOUTH AND MOVED ON AND ON. APEX AND HIS CREW WERE AT SOUTH POINT AND APEX AND SOUTH POINT PRINCE WERE FRIENDS FROM THEIR CHILDHOOD SO APEX HAS NOTHING TO WORRY ABOUT. APEX FIRST THOUGHT TO FIND DANE SO HE KEPT SEARCHING FOR HIM FOR HOURS AND HOURS. APEX FOUND DANE WITH THE HELP OF HIS CREW. APEX TOLD DANE EVERYTHING AND DANE EVEN THOUGHT THAT THIS IS A JACKPOT. SO BOTH OF THEM SEARCHED FOR HENRY AND FINALLY INSIDE A BAR THEY FOUND HENRY. DANE TOLD HENRY THAT "MORNINGSTAR DID SO MANY CRIMES IN WEST SIGHT AND NOW WE NEED TO FIND HIM AT ANY COST SO WE NEED YOU TO HELP US AND WE CAN PAY YOU 3000 GOLD COINS FOR THAT".HENRY ACCEPTED AND ALSO TOLD HIM TO NOT TO THINK OF BETRAYING HIM. APEX AND DANE TOLD OK. NOW BOTH DANE AND APEX WITH HENRY WENT ON A BIG SHIP TOWARDS NORTH WITH OVER 50 MEMBERS CREW. APEX TOLD YOU WHY YOU WENT SOUTH TO FIND MORNINGSTAR WHEN MORNINGSTAR IS AT NORTH. AND WHY DIDN‘T I ENCOUNTER HIM WITH MY EYES? HENRY TOLD ME THAT HE TRICKED ME BY SAYING LIKE THAT. HE NEVER DOES THE THING HE SAYS AND WE NEED MORE PEOPLE TO DEFEAT HIM. APEX SAID WHY DO WE NEED MORE? WE HAVE THE BEST SHIP WITH 50 PEOPLE. WHY YOU ARE FEARED TO FACE HIM? HENRY TOLD THAT "CAPT. MORNINGSTAR IS NOT AS YOU THOUGHT. HE ALWAYS WEARS

SHARK

THE SKULL OF A GREAT WHITE SHARK AS A CROWN AND HE WEARS A BROKEN TOOTH OF A KILLER WHALE TO YOUR SURPRISE HE KILLED THAT SHARK AT AT THE AGE OF 8 AND HE TOOK THE KILLER WHALE’S TOOTH AT 12. HE WAS DECLARED TO BE DEAD FOR 3 TIMES IN 1673,1666 AND 1642, BUT TO OUR SURPRISE HE CAME BACK".NO ONE KNOWS HIS REAL NAME ALL CALL HIM WITH IS 2ND NAME "MORNINGSTAR" AFTER HIS DAD'S DDEATHHE CALLS HIMSELF LIKE THAT EXCEPT HIMSELF NO ONE KNOWS HIS NAME INCLUDING HIS ONE LIVING WIFE ON LAND AND HIS SON TOO.

CHAPTER II

Captain Morningstar

HERE MICHAEL WAS ON LAND SEARCHING AND ASKING PEOPLE ABOUT MORNINGSTAR BUT THEN A GROUP OF PEOPLE ATTACKED ON THE PLACE WHERE WAS. MICHAEL BY SEEING THEM UNDERSTOOD THAT THEY WERE SENT BY KING LUCAS FROM THE "RED HOUSE" KINGDOM.

A GIRL SLIGHTLY OPENED HER DOOR AND ASKED FOR MICHAEL TO COME IN AND MICHAEL WENT IN THERE. AFTER A FEW HOURS ALL WENT FROM THERE. THE GIRL SAID SHE IS CLOE AND MICHAEL INTRODUCED HIMSELF AND HE ASKED HER ABOUT MORNINGSTAR. CLOE ASKED HIM "ARE YOU GOING TO KILL HIM" THEN MICHAEL TOLD YES AND THEN CLOE STEPPED BACK AND MOVED RIGHT. MICHAEL UNDERSTOOD THAT SHE WANTS HE DO NOT SEE THE LETTER ON THE DESK SO HE GRABBED THE LETTER AND TO HIS SURPRISE IT WAS FROM CAPTAIN MORNINGSTAR SAYS HE WILL RETURN TO LAND AFTER GETTING RID OF HENRY AND HE WROTE FROM YOUR LOVINGLY HUSBAND MORNINGSTAR. MICHAEL UNDERSTOOD THAT CLOE IS THE WIFE OF MORNINGSTAR BUT HE WAS A GOOD MAN SO HE DIDN'T USE HIS HAND AND ASKED HER POLITELY. SHE TOLD ME THAT SHE DOES KNOW WHERE HE WILL GO AND SHE ALSO TOLD "HE COMES ONCE IN EVERY 4 YEARS TO ME". HE IS A GOOD PERSON AS WELL AS A BEAST TOO. MORNINGSTAR WANTS TO KILL LUCAS BECAUSE OUR KING RONAN IS GOT

MURDERED BY LUCAS. LUCAS WANTS RONAN'S KINGDOM "UTOPIA" AND LUCAS KILLED HALF OF THE POPULATION OF UTOPIA. MORNINGSTAR WILL KILL LUCAS TOMORROW. MICHAEL RUSHES TOWARDS THE SOUTH WITH CLOE BECAUSE MICHAEL KNOWS THAT THERE IS MORE INFORMATION HE NEEDS. NOW MICHAEL WITH A CREW BOAT IN AN HOUR GOES TOWARDS THE SOUTH AND FINALLY, HE FINDS APEX AS WELL AS DANE TO. THE TRIP WAS TERRIFYING FOR MICHAEL. THEY BOTH TELL EVERYTHING TO MICHAEL BUT THEN MICHAEL SHIP GETS SHOTTED BY ANOTHER SHIP AND THAT SHIP WAS "BROWN WOODS". CAPTAIN MORNINGSTAR CAME TO KILL HENRY. HENRY HERE KEPT THE KNIFE ON APEX NECK AND TOLD THE CREW TO ATTACK. HENRY'S CREW TIED MICHAEL, DEAN, APEX, AND CLOE ON MICHAEL'S SHIP AND THEY ESCAPED AND ATTACKED ON MORNINGSTAR BUT MORNINGSTAR WAS TOO POWERFUL AND DEFENDED HIMSELF AND HENRY'S SHIP WAS BLASTED.

Enter Caption

MORNINGSTAR RESCUED APEX, DEAN, MICHAEL, AND HIS WIFE CLOE. MICHAEL SAID TO MORNINGSTAR THAT HE KNOWS HIS NEXT MOVE AND THAT'S NOT GONNA WORK. MORNINGSTAR ASKED WHAT IS MY NEXT MOVE THEN MICHAEL TOLD HIM THAT YOU ARE GOING TO KILL LUCAS AND I ALREADY SENT HIM A MESSAGE THROUGH MY

PIDGEON THEN MORNINGSTAR REPLIED "EVEN I DON'T KNOW THAT MY NEXT MOVE IS TO KILL LUCAS I JUST GO RANDOM AND I WILL KNOW OTHERS NEXT MOVES AND YOU KNOW WHAT LUCAS NEXT MOVE IS TO RAID WEST SIGHT AND KILL WILLIAM. HE IS ATTACKING THROUGH THE SEA" APEX TELLS HIM THAT WE NEED TO STOP HIM THEN CAPTAIN MORNINGSTAR TELLS YOU SHOULD GO TOWARDS WEST SIGHT AND I WILL COME THERE LATER. THEN 4 OF THEM TOOK MICHAEL'S SHIP AND WENT TO WEST SIGHT. MORNINGSTAR WANTS MORE CREW SO HE WENT TO SOUTH WEST WHERE HE CAN FIND SOME PEOPLE TO WORK FOR HIM ON HIS SHIP FOR THEIR WHOLE LIFE. CAPT. MORNINGSTAR FOUND SOME PEOPLE TO WORK WITH HIM ON HIS SHIP.

HERE APEX TOLD DEAN AND MICHAEL TO STAY AND NOT COME TO THE PALACE CAUSE WILLIAM MAY HAVE GOTTEN THE NEWS ABOUT US TEAMING UP WITH A PIRATE. THEN APEX GOES TO THE KINGDOM AND SAYS WILLIAM THAT LUCAS IS COMING TO KILL HIM AND HE STARTS TO SAY BAD THINGS ABOUT LUCAS. THE THINGS HE WAS TELLING WERE TRUE BUT WILLIAM DID NOT KNOW THE TRUTH SO HE YELLED AT APEX AND SAID APEX TO RETURN. APEX CAME OUT ANGRILY, HE WENT TO DEAN AND TOLD THE WHOLE STORY. MICHAEL WAS NOT THERE, APEX ASKED ABOUT MICHAEL AND DEAN SAID THAT HE WENT TO THE KINGDOM BECAUSE YOU WERE LATE. APEX SAID THAT WILLIAM IS IN A BAD MODE AND HE MAY YELL AT MICHAEL TOO... AND IN MINUTES THEY RUSHED TO THE PALACE TO STOP MICHAEL. HERE MICHAEL WAS

CALM AND HE DID NOT TELL WILLIAM ABOUT LUCAS CAUSE HE CAME TO KNOW THAT LUCAS IS COMING TO VISIT THE PALACE AND IF HE TALKS BAD ABOUT LUCAS AT THIS POINT THEN HE MAY GET PUNISHED. AFTER A FEW HOURS LUCAS'S BROTHER MIKE CAME AND TOLD HIM THAT LUCAS IS NOT THERE BECAUSE OF HIS URGENT WORK AND MIKE GAVE SOME GOLD AND PRESENTS TO WILLIAM FOR THE ABSENCE OF HIS BROTHER. WILLIAM WITHOUT QUESTION TOOK MIKE AROUND HIS PALACE BY HIMSELF. MICHAEL WAS BACK OF WILLIAM WATCHING MIKE AND MIKE DID NOT KNOW THAT MICHAEL IS KEEPING AN EYE ON HIM. AFTER A FEW MINUTES OF TOUR MIKE SLOWLY GRABBED HIS DAGGER AND LUCKILY MICHAEL SAW IT SO HE PUSHED MIKE AWAY AND HE SAVED WILLIAM. MIKE FELL APART AND HIS DAGGER IS VISIBLE TO ALL THE PEOPLE IN THE PLACE. WILLIAM WAS SURPRISED BY SEEING THE DAGGER. HE CALLS HIS KNIGHT NAMED SULPHURIC. HE TELLS HIM TO TAKE MIKE TO THE PUNISHMENT CHAMBER AND TELLS MICHAEL TO CALL APEX. MICHAEL GOES OUT AND ON THE WAY HE FINDS APEX AND DEAN SO THEY 3 TOGETHER WENT TO THE PALACE AND THEY ENTERED THE PUNISHMENT CHAMBER. MIKE WAS GETTING KILLED BY WILLIAM AND AFTER A FEW MINUTES MIKE HEAD WAS CUT OFF. THIS INFORMATION WENT TO LUCAS AND LUCAS SENT WILLIAM A LETTER.

CHAPTER III

The Letter By Lucas

DEAR WILLIAM,

YOUR KINGDOM IS FAMOUS FOR YOUR SHIPS SO I CHALLENGE YOU FOR A WAR BRING YOUR
SHIPS AND I WILL PROVE THAT MY SHIPS ARE STRONGER THAN YOURS AND I WILL OCCUPY YOUR LAND AND NAME IT ON MY BROTHER'S NAME.

YOURS SINCERELY,
EMPEROR LUCAS THE GREAT.

CHAPTER IV

The Sea War

WILLIAM AND LUCAS BOTH WERE READY WITH THEIR SHIPS AND AT THIS POINT IT WAS A BIG WAR. WITH 90 AND 90 SHIPS AND 700 AND 700 PEOPLE ON EACH SIDE. THE WAR STARTED AND AFTER A FEW HOURS WILLIAM'S SHIPS WERE GETTING DOWN SLOWLY. WILLIAM IS SAD AND HE IS THINKING TO GIVE UP, BUT HE RULED WEST SIGHT FOR 30 YEARS AND HIS FATHER, GRANDFATHER, GREAT GRANDFATHER, AND GREAT GREAT GRANDFATHER RULED WEST SIGHT FOR OVER 370 YEARS AND NOW HE WANTED TO GIVE THE KINGDOM TO ONE OF HIS SONS. THE ONLY THING ABOUT WEST SIGHT IS THAT FOR 370 YEARS ITS NAME AND NOT BEEN CHANGED. WILLIAM THINKS A LOT AND AFTER A FEW MINUTES HE SAYS TO ATTACK FROM THE BACK, BUT IT WAS NOT USEFUL. HE LOST OVER 300 PEOPLE AND 50 SHIPS. WILLIAM DON'T KNOW WHAT TO DO BUT THEN SOME SHIP TOOK LUCAS'S SHIPS DOWN ONE AFTER ONE. WHEN APEX SAW IT CAREFULLY IT WAS CAPTAIN MORNINGSTAR.

LUCAS IS TOO POWERFUL AND MORNINGSTAR KNEW IT SO HE THOUGHT TO TRICK HIM. MORNINGSTAR HAD A PLAN. HE THOUGHT ABOUT SURRENDERING HIMSELF TO LUCAS AND AT THE RIGHT TIME HE THOUGHT TO KILL HIM. AND THEN SUDDENLY WHILE HE WAS THINKING FROM NOWHERE HEARD A WHISTLE. IT WAS A SHIP, A SHIP WHICH IS KNOWN TO MORNINGSTAR. IT WAS THE

SHIP OF CAPTAIN HENRY. HENRY WASN'T DEAD. HERE APEX WAS ALSO SHOCKED BY SEEING HENRY ALIVE. APEX SHOUTED SAYING LUCAS, HENRY, AND MORNINGSTAR TO TALK ON LAND THEN THREE OF THEM CAME TO THE LAND, AND THEN LUCAS SAID THAT AT ANY COST HE WILL KILL WILLIAM THEN MORNINGSTAR TOLD: "I WILL SURRENDER TO YOU AND BY TOMORROW WILLIAM WILL BE AT YOUR KINGDOM AND THEN YOU RELEASE ME, AND FREE WEST SIGHT." LUCAS SAID OK BUT APEX SAID NO. NOW IT WAS A PROBLEM FOR THEM BUT MORNINGSTAR SOMEHOW MADE APEX ACCEPT THE OFFER AND TOLD HIM TO BRING WILLIAM TOMORROW. MORNINGSTAR WENT WITH LUCAS AND HENRY WANTED MORNINGSTAR TO DIE, SO HE THOUGHT TO ATTACK HIM WHEN WILLIAM COMES AND MORNINGSTAR GETS FREE. APEX WENT TO WILLIAM AND EXPLAINED EVERYTHING WHILE THERE ARE SAILING BACK WEST SIGHT. WILLIAM WANT TO SAVE WEST SIGHT SO HE ANNOUNCED THE APEX AS THE NEW KING AND ACCEPTED THE HIS DEATH. HERE MORNINGSTAR WAS IN A JAIL DOWN THE SHIP. HE WAS IN SEARCH OF THE OPPORTUNITY TO KILL LUCAS. HE LOOKED AROUND AND SAW THAT THERE IS A AXE NEARBY AND IF HE HAD SOMETHING LONG ENOUGH HE CAN EASILY REACH THAT AXE AND BREAK THE PRISON. THE PRISON IS BREAKABLE, NOT WITH BARE HANDS BUT WITH AN AXE. HE GRABBED THAT AXE BY TAKING THE NEARBY STICK AND TYING IT TO HIS LONG HAIR, BUT IT WAS NOT LONG ENOUGH SO HE TOOK OFF HIS HAT AND HE TORE THEM, AND MADE THEM INTO LONG FABRICS. HE TORE HIS DRESS AND AT THE LAST HE TIED IT

TO A STICK AND HE THREW IT NEAR THE AXE AND MADE THAT AXE FALLS APART AND BRINGS IT NEAR HIM. AFTER IT CAME TO A DISTANCE HE KEPT HIS ONE LEG OUT AND WITH HIS LEG FINGERS HE MADE THAT AXE COME NEAR. AFTER THAT HE JUST TOOK THAT AXE AND KEPT IT WITH HIM. AT MIDNIGHT WHEN HE THOUGHT IT WAS THE RIGHT TIME SO HE SILENTLY CUT THAT PRISON BAR AND AFTER 1 AND HALF HOURS OF CUTTING HE FINALLY BROKE TWO BARS AND THAT WAS ENOUGH IF HE TRY. HE CAME OUT AND WENT TO LUCAS ROOM AND HE SNEAKED. WHEN HE ENTERED HIS ROOM BY CRAWLING ON THE GROUND LUCAS SAID MORNINGSTAR TO WAKE UP. MORNINGSTAR WAS SHOCKED CAUSE NO ONE EVER KNEW HIS PLAN HE JUST GOES RANDOM ACCORDING TO THE SURROUNDINGS. HE JUST KEEPS A CONTENT IN HIS MIND AND EXECUTES THE CONTENT HE WANTS TO DO WITH THE HELP OF THINGS AROUND HIM. LUCAS SAID "MORNINGSTAR IS A MAN WITH PRIDE. HE JUST THINKS ABOUT HIMSELF." NO YELLED MORNINGSTAR. LUCAS SAID THAT HE NEVER CARED ABOUT HIS WIFE OR HIS SON. HE ALWAYS DID ROBBERIES, MURDERS, AND ALL CRIMES AND HE WANTS TO KILL LUCAS BECAUSE PEOPLE FROM MORNINGSTAR AREA WERE AFRAID OF LUCAS AND NOT MORNINGSTAR WHICH WASN'T NICE TO MORNINGSTAR. THEN MORNINGSTAR RAISED HIS AXE AND TRIED TO ATTACK LUCAS, BUT MORNINGSTAR GOT STABBED IN HIS BACK. WHEN HE TURNED AROUND HE SAW DANE. LET ME TELL YOU A SMALL STORY ABOUT A LION SAID DANE. DANE AGAIN SAID THAT ONCE THERE USED TO BE A LION, TIGER, AND LEOPARD. THEY TOGETHER STAYED

HAPPILY BUT ONE DAY THE DAY TO CHOOSE THE KING OF THE JUNGLE OLD KING CHOSE TIGER AND THEN LION GOT FRUSTRATED. LION GOT NOTHING, HE WANTED TO FIND A SUNKEN CITY ON WHICH HE WANTED TO RULE AND HE RESEARCHED ON IT FOR YEARS BUT NOW HE WAS NOT A KING SO HE CHOSE THE ANOTHER WAY. TO TEAM UP WITH HEYNS. HERE LION IS ME, TIGER IS THE APEX, JUNGLE IS WEST SIGHT AND THE SUNKEN CITY IS ATLANTIS.

CHAPTER V

Atlantis

ATLANTIS

MORNINGSTAR WAS SURPRISED. HE THOUGHT THAT IT WAS A LIE BUT DANE HAD SOMETHING WHICH CAN PROVE THAT ATLANTIS EXISTS. HE HAD A PAINTING OF ATLANTIS AND THEIR PEOPLE, AND KINGDOM AS WELL AS HE HAD SOME HAND SCRIPTS OF ATLANTIS. DANE TOLD THAT MORNINGSTAR IS GOING TO HELP HIM TO FIND ATLANTIS BUT MORNINGSTAR SAID NO. DANE HAD MORNINGSTAR'S WIFE SO MORNINGSTAR NEEDED TO ACCEPT IT. MORNINGSTAR TOLD THAT ATLANTIS IS SUNKEN ACCORDING TO TALES THEN WHY DO YOU NEED

THAT? THEN DANE TOLD THAT HE WANTED TO RULE IT BY BRINGING IT UP ON LAND AND MAKING IT STAND BY USING SPELLS OF "THE CODEX GIGAS " ALSO KNOWN AS THE DEVIL'S BIBLE BUT HE COULD NOT SO HE THOUGHT TO STEAL THE TREASURE OF ATLANTIS. MORNINGSTAR WANTED TO ASK MORE QUESTIONS BUT DANE TOLD NO AND TOLD HIM TO GET ON WITH HIS WORK. THEY TURNED THEIR SHIP BACK AND THE NEXT DAY WILLIAM WAS AT LUCAS'S KINGDOM BUT LUCAS WAS NOT THERE SO HE JUST WAITED. CAPTAIN MORNINGSTAR WAS THINKING ABOUT ATLANTIS. DANE TOLD MORNINGSTAR TO GO TO NORTH WEST.

MORNINGSTAR WANTED TO TELL APEX BUT HE CAN'T. DANE WAS CURIOUS TO STEAL ATLANTIS WEALTH. DANE, HENRY, AND MORNINGSTAR WERE ON THE LAND AND THEY HAD THERE 40 MEMBERS CREW. MORNINGSTAR ASKED DANE WHERE ARE THEY GOING BECAUSE THEY WERE GOING ON LAND. DANE TELLS THAT THEY ARE GOING TOWARDS DYANAS, THE MIGHTIEST ARMY ON THIS PLANET. MORNINGSTAR TOLD THAT THEY NEED AT LEAST 20KG GOLD PER 1 MAN AND HOW MANY ARE WE GOING TO HIRE? JUST 150 REPLIED DANE. MORNINGSTAR WAS SHOCKED, AND HE ASKED HIM "FROM WHERE YOU WILL PAY FOR THEM?" THE WEALTH OF ATLANTIS TOLD DANE. AFTER HOURS OF WALKING THEY WERE FINALLY AT DYANAS, BUT ALL THE DYANAS WERE HIRED, AND NO MORE WERE LEFT FOR THEM, EXCEPT ONE.

AMICA DYANA

THE GIRL WHO KILLED OVER 12,000 PEOPLE, BY WHOSE NAME PEOPLE, KNIGHTS, KINGS, AND EVEN EMPEROR GEORGE WERE AFRAID OF. HER NAME WAS

AMEICA SERIAS. DANE ASKED AMICA THAT SHE REALLY KILLED 12,000 PEOPLE. SHE TOLD THAT SHE KILLED 12,747 PEOPLE EXACTLY AND SHE WAS HIRED BY 3000 VARIOUS KINGS AND THEY GAVE HER OVER 300,000 TONS OF GOLD SHE TOLD THAT SHE NEEDS OVER 70KG GOLD PER DAY. DANE ACCEPTED IT CAUSE SHE WAS EQUAL TO GOD SO HE BELIEVED THAT 70 GOLD ARE WORTH IT. THEY ALL WENT TOWARDS THEIR SHIP BACK AND WITHIN ONE DAY THEY WERE ON THEIR SHIP. THEY WENT TOWARDS ATLANTIS AND FINALLY, THEY WERE 20KM AWAY FROM ATLANTIS, BUT NOW DANE DOESN'T KNOW THE CORRECT ROUTE TOWARDS ATLANTIS. HE WAS UNABLE TO RECOGNIZE IT. CAPTAIN MORNINGSTAR TOLD THAT "WHAT IF WE WANT SOMETHING TO FIND THE ROUTE FOR ATLANTIS." DANE REPLIED, "WE WANT CODEX GIGAS, THE DEVIL'S BIBLE.

Enter Caption

"MORNINGSTAR TOLD THAT WHY WE NEED THAT. AND HOW DO YOU KNOW THAT WE NEED IT?

ATLANTIS WAS SUNKEN SEVERAL YEARS AGO AND PEOPLE DON'T KNOW THE EXACT PLACE WHERE IT SUNK, ACCORDING TO MY KNOWLEDGE CODEX GIGAS HAS A SPELL WHICH WHEN CAST GIVES US WHAT WE WANT FROM OUR HEARTS. BUT TO REACH IT WE NEED TO KNOW WHERE IT IS AND IF YOU THINK IT IS IN KINGDOM CEECAVE YOU ARE WRONG CAUSE IT IS A COPY, THE ORIGINAL ONE IS PRESENT IN A RIDDLE AND WE NEED TO SOLVE IT.

"IN BETWEEN OF TWO OCEANS, THE UNSEEN DEAD END APPEARS FOR EVERY 100-YEARS IF YOU WANT THE GIGAS BUT BEWARE OF HYENAS HIDING"

MORNINGSTAR TELLS THAT IT IS EASY, WHICH MEANS THAT GIGAS IS LOCATED IN THE CENTRE OF 2 OCEANS WHICH IS UNSEEN AND APPEARS EVERY 100 YEARS. THEN DANE ASKS ABOUT HYENAS PRESENT IN IT AND MORNINGSTAR COULDN'T ANSWER IT. AFTER A WHILE OF THINKING MORNINGSTAR SAYS THAT THEY NEED TO GO TO THE EAST CAUSE HEYNAS LIVES IN THE EAST IN SAVANAS. THEN DANE TELLS WHERE IT WOULD BE IN SAVANA CAUSE SAVANA IS

DOUBLE THE SIZE OF WEST SIGHT. IT IS INSIDE A FEMALE HYENA BECAUSE 60 PERCENT OF BABY HYENAS SUFFOCATE WHILE THEY ARE COMING OUT TOLD MORNINGSTAR. THEY ALL RUSHED TOWARD SAVANA IN THE HOPE TO FIND IT, AND FINALLY, AFTER REACHING SAVANA THEY STARTED TO MOVE A LITTLE INSIDE SO THEY CAN FIND SOME HYENAS. AFTER QUITE A TIME DANE ASKS HOW CAN WE FIND THE ONE HEYNA WITH CODEX GIGAS. THE HYENA WHICH GIVES BIRTH TO ITS YOUNG ONES IN THE AFTERNOON WHEN THE SUN IS ABOVE US THE

PLACE WHERE IT GIVES BIRTH WILL HAVE THE CODEX GIGAS ANSWERS MORNINGSTAR. "YOU TOLD ME THAT IT IS INSIDE OF HEYNA AND NOW YOU ARE TELLING IT IS BURIED ARE YOU SURE ABOUT IT? CAUSE I FEEL SOMETHING FISHY". NOT EXACTLY, BUT ACCORDING TO THE RIDDLE IT SHOULD HAPPEN EVERY 100 YEARS, AND THE CODEX WAS WRITTEN IN THE 13TH CENTURY AND THERE ARE VERY LESS HYENAS BECAUSE OF LESS BREEDING, SO THE ONE WHICH IS PREGNANT IS THE 0NE WITH THE GIGAS REPLIES MORNINGSTAR. THEY ALL WITHIN HOURS FIND OUT THE ONLY PREGNANT FEMALE HEYNA. AFTER 3 DAYS OF LIVING IN THE SAVANA AND LOOKING AFTER THEIR HEYNA IT WAS THE TIME FOR HEYNA'S DELIVERY.

HYENA HAD A DEAD CHILD AND AFTER A FEW HOURS OF EXTREME PAIN THE HYENA DELIVERS 3 CHILDREN OF WHICH 2 WERE ALIVE AND 1 WAS DEAD. MORNINGSTAR AND HIS TEAM WENT TOWARDS THE DEAD HYENA AND STARTED DIGGING THERE FOR CODEX GIGAS AND AFTER DIGGING OVER 4 FEET DOWN THEY FOUND NOTHING. AMICA TELLS THAT THEY NEED TO SEE IN THE CAVE WHERE THE 2 SURVIVING CHILDREN ARE HIDDEN, IT MAY WORK AND SHE TOOK A FEW MEMBERS WITH HER. DANE TOLD THAT THEY SHOULD START DIGGING MORE IN THE HOPE OF FINDING CODEX GIGAS. AMICA WAS AT HER DESTINATION AND SHE SLOWLY MOVED ON. SHE WAITED FOR A FEW MINS AND SHE FINALLY AFTER THE FEMALE HYENA LEFT THE CAVE SHE WENT IN. SHE SAW THAT ONE OF THAT BABY HYENA WAS DEAD. SHE MARKED THAT PLACE AND WENT BACK TO MORNINGSTAR. DANE SAW AMICA AND ASKED

WHAT HAPPENED. SHE TOLD THAT TO COME WITH HER SO THAT THEY CAN DIG THE PLACE WHERE ANOTHER HYENA CHILD DIED. OHH!!!! DID ONE OF THAT DID BABY DIE? LEAVE IT... YOU TELL THAT WHY YOU THINK CODEX GIGAS IS PRESENT THAT CAVE SAID MORNINGSTAR AMICA TOLD THAT THE CAVE IS IN MIDDLE OF TWO OCEANS AND IF YOU SEE IT CAREFULLY THAT HYENA AS HIDING IN THE CAVE BUT NOT THIS HYENA WHICH WAS DEAD NEAR A BEACH OR NEAR OCEAN COAST. THEY ALL WENT TO THAT CAVE AND STARTED DIGGING IN. AFTER DIGGING FOR 3 FEET THEY FINALLY FOUND A CHEST AND WHEN THEY OPENED IT, THEY SAW A BOOK WITH SATAN PICTURE ON IT. IT WAS CODEX GIGAS. AFTER THIS MANY STRUGGLES FINALLY CODEX GIGAS WAS FOUND NOW THEY NEED TO GO TO ATLANTIS AND FIND ITS WEALTH, BUT MORNINGSTAR SAYS TODANE THAT THEY CAN BRING ATLANTIS TO THE SURFACE AND MAKE IT A KINGDOM.YES!!!! I CAN RULE IT, I CAN BE A KING AS I WANT AND I CAN OWN WEST SIGHT TOO... SAID DANE. WAIT WHAT DO YOU MEAN BY YOU CAN OWN IT? YOU KNOW THAT YOU KIDNAPPED MY WIFE, BUT I WAS ONLY WITH YOU BECAUSE OF YOUR DEAL OF 25 PERCENT OF THE WEALTH AND NOW YOU ARE TELLING ME YOU WILL RULE... YOU KNOW THAT YOU ARE NOT ELIGIBLE FOR THAT. YOU CAN'T RULE ATLANTIS, THE ONLY PERSON WHO CAN RULE IT IS ME. I AM DIFFERENT FROM ALL YOU ARE JUST A TINY BRATIN IN FRONT OF ME. I HAVE THE WORLD'S FASTEST SHIP WITH THE WORLD'S BEST FIGHTING SKILLS. COME!! FIGHT WITH ME AND WIN ATLANTIS SAID MORNINGSTAR. DANE TAKES HIS SWORD OUT

AND AIMS AT MORNINGSTAR AND STRIKES ON HIM. MORNINGSTAR DODGES IT AND STRIKES BACK AGAIN. AMICA WAS READING CODEX GIGAS. DANE TAKES A FRONT STEP AND WIPES MORNINGSTAR'S EYE OFF. MORNINGSTAR SHOUTS IN PAIN, HE YELLS HARD. MORNINGSTAR WAS FEELING WEAK. DANE TELLS HIS CREW TO TAKE MORNINGSTAR AND TIE HIM NAKED ON THE TOP OF BROWN WOOD.

CHAPTER VI

The End [Or] The Beginning

DANE WAS GOING TOWARDS NORTH SO THEY CAN GET CORAL REEFS, BECAUSE FOR CASTING THE SPELL WHICH MAKES ATLANTIS COME TO THE GROUND AND FIND ITS ROUTE NEEDS CORAL REEFS, SHARK TEETH, AND SOME SIMPLE THINGS AVAILABLE IN WATER LIKE GOLDFISH,
SAND ETC. DANE WAS SLEEPING IN HIS ROOM AND THEN FROM NOWHERE IN NO TIME A NAKED MAN ATTACKED ON DANE, BUT DANE REFLEXES WERE SO GOOD THAT HE EASILY ESCAPED IT. AND THE NAKED WAS OBVIOUSLY MORNINGSTAR. WHO SOMEHOW ESCAPED FROM THE TOP AND TRIED TO ASSASSINATE DANE. DANE TOLD THAT MORNINGSTAR CAN NOT DO ANYTHING CAUSE HE IS VERY PUNY. MORNINGSTAR SAID "YOU ARE PUNY NOT ME. YOU ARE NOT ME, I AM THE PERFECT KING, PIRATE, AND THE BEST FIGHTER. YOU ARE A REJECTED PIECE WHO CAME OUT FROM HIS KINGDOM, WHO WAS BORN TO BE A KING BUT DID NOT BE." BY LISTENING TO THIS DANE TOLD "YOU ARE THINKING THAT ALTHEN IS YOUR DAD, BUT DID YOU KNOW THAT YOU WERE A NAKED, HARMED, THE DIRTY CHILD FELL IN THE TRASH AND WAS ADOPTED BY A THIEF. YOUR WHOLE LIFE IS A LIE!!! I KNOW MORE ABOUT YOUR LIFE THAN YOU DO. YOUR SON ISN‘T YOUR SON. YOUR WIFE CHEATED ON YOU AND THAT IS BECAUSE OF YOUR PRIDE... I THINK YOU REMEMBER THAT YOU DIDN’T LOVE HER... I KNOW THAT YOU

MARRIED HER FOR WEALTH, BUT CLOE LOVED YOU AND THAT IS WHY SHE LEFT HER FATHER AND CAME WITH YOU, BUT YOU WANT HER WEALTH NOT HER LOVE SO YOU JUST LEFT HER, ACTED LIKE YOU LOVE HER AND EVEN CLOE KNOWS IT. YOUR FATHER ADOPTED YOU TO MAKE YOU A SLAVE. YOU WERE BORN TO BE A SLAVE NOT A CAPTAIN OR A KING, YOU ARE A FREAKING SLAVE. THE ATTACK OF OTHER PIRATES MADE YOUR BROTHERS DIE AND YOU WERE THE ONLY REMAINING CHILD WHO ALSO WASN'T A REAL CHILD, HE WAS ADOPTED AND UNLUCKILY HE GAVE CAPTAINCY TO YOU AND DIED IN THAT ATTACK." AND TAKES OUT HIS DAGGER AND STUBBS IN THE STOMACH OF MORNINGSTAR. AND WITHIN SECONDS A BIG ATTACK FROM NOWHERE ON THEIR SHIP COMES. THEY DESTROYED THE WHOLE BROWN WOOD AND THE SHIP WHICH DESTROYED BROWN WOOD, THE WORLD'S FASTEST THE SHIP WAS BROWN LOG. A SHIP THAT IS NEW AND IS FASTER THAN BROWN WOOD. IT WAS OWNED BY A MAN WHO WAS KNOWN TO ALL. HE WAS APEX WITH HIS FORCE.

APEX BLASTS BROWN WOOD AND MAKES IT BREAK INTO PIECES. APEX SEES CLOE IN THE DISTANCE, SUFFERING TO STAY ALIVE IN BETWEEN THE OCEAN. HE HELPS HER OUT AND HE ALSO HELPS THE OTHER CREWMATES. WHEN HE WAS ABOVE TO TAK EA TURN, HE SAW A GUY NAKED AND FLOATING ON A PLANK. HE WASHURTED AND WAS BLEEDING A LOT AND THAT MAN WAS NOT ANOTHER THAN CAPTAIN MORNINGSTAR. HE BRINGS HIM UP, WAKES HIM UP, AND GIVES HIM CLOTHES AS WELL AS A FEW MEDICINES. HE ASKS HIM "HOW HE CAME TO DANE'S

SHIP "AND HE ANSWERS HOW HE CAME. APEX SAYS THAT HE IS SAD ABOUT DANE, BUT ALSO ANGRY CAUSE WILLIAM TOLD HIM ABOUT DANE. MORNINGSTAR SEES AMICA ON THE SHIP AND COMES TO KNOW THAT SHE IS ALSO ALIVE. HE TALKS WITH HER AND FINALLY, ALL OF THEM WENT TO THEIR HOMES. AMICA TO SAVANA, APEX, AND MICHAEL TO WEST SIGHT, MORNINGSTAR, AND CLOE TO THEIR HOME. MORNINGSTAR LIVES 1 MONTH WITH HIS WIFE

AND ONE DAY WHEN HE WAS AT A BAR, A DRUNKEN MAN INTRODUCES HIMSELF AS JOHN TO MORNINGSTAR AND HE STARTS TELLING A STORY. HE SAID A STORY ABOUT HIS AND MORNINGSTAR'S WIFE'S DATE. HE TELLS HER THAT SHE IS IN LOVE WITH HIM NOT MORNINGSTAR. MORNINGSTAR CALMLY GOES TO HIS HOUSE AND ASKS HER WIFE AND AS IN ALL CASES SHE TELLS HIM SHE DID NOT DO IT, BUT HE KEEPS ON ASKING FOR A WHILE AND CLOE YELLS AT HIM SAYING "WHY ARE YOU TORTURING ME? DO YOU TRUST ME OR JOHN? WHY ARE YOU FRUSTRATING ME? MORNINGSTAR DID NOT TELL ANYTHING ABOUT JOHN AND HE DID NOT EVEN TAKE HIS NAME. HE UNDERSTOOD THAT HIS WIFE CHEATED ON HIM. HE QUIETLY WENT BACK TO THE OCEAN AND HE WROTE A LETTER TO THE APEX AND ASKED HIM FOR A SHIP FOR THE HELP HE DID. HE REQUESTED HIM. HERE CLOE WAS PREGNANT AND WAS

HAVING A 15-DAY-OLD CHILD IN HER STOMACH AND NO ONE KNEW IT, EVEN HERSELF. MORNINGSTAR GOT BROWN LOG FROM APEX AS A HE REQUESTED. HE FOUND A CREW AND WITH HIS LAST LITTLE

MONEY HE HIRED A CREW.

AFTER 7 MONTHS........

APEX RECEIVES A LETTER FROM THE SOUTH COAST SAYING THAT THEY SAY SOME DISTURBANCE IN THE WATER. APEX WAS SHOCKED!!! WHY WOULD BE THERE A

DISTURBANCE IN THE WATER? HE DID NOT GET ANY COMPLAINTS LIKE THAT DURING HIS CHILDHOOD. HE WENT THERE AND HE SAW THE WHOLE PLACE. ONCE HE WENT BACK OFF THE MOUNTAIN, HE SAW A SWORD PIERCED INTO A ROCK.

Enter Caption

CHAPTER VII

A New Start

HE AS FAST AS HE CAN, CALLED HIS KNIGHT AND TOLD HIM TO SEND A LETTER TO MICHAEL AND MORNINGSTAR TELLING THEM TO COME. MICHAEL WAS RULING A UTOPIA AFTER LUCAS DEATH CAUSED AT ONE POINT APEX AND MICHAEL BOTH TOGETHER KILLED LUCAS SO APEX HELD UTOPIA IN THE HANDS OF MICHAEL AND AS ALWAYS CAPTAIN MORNINGSTAR IS DOING SOME ROBBERIES WITH HIS CREWMATES. THEY BOTH CAME TO APEX AND MICHAEL ASKED HIM "WHY DO YOU CALL US BROTHER?" DANE IS BACK. WHEN I WAS 14 YEARS OLD I GAVE HIM A SWORD WITH HE CARRIED UNTIL HIS DEATH. IT WAS A SWORD OF WILLIAM, WHICH HE GOT AS A GIFT. IT BRINGS LUCK TO THE FIGHTER AND THAT'S WHY DANE CARRIED IT UNTIL HIS DEATH AND I GAVE HIM IT BECAUSE HE WAS SAD ON THE DAY I WON. I SAW THIS SWORD IN THE HANDS OF DANE WHILE I KILLED HIM AND I SAW IT YESTERDAY ON A MOUNTAIN REPLIED APEX. WE NEED TO KILL HIM BEFORE HE GETS CODEX GIGAS TOLD MORNINGSTAR. WHAT!!!!

CODEX GIGAS IS STILL THERE? DIDN'T IT GET DESTROYED IN THE BLAST? TOLD APEX. IT IS WITH AMICA TOLD MORNINGSTAR. MICHAEL ASKED, "HOW YOU KNOW?" SHE IS VERY CLOSE TO ME REPLIED MORNINGSTAR. THEY THREE TOGETHER WITH 4 SHIPS AND 120 PEOPLE WENT

TO SAVANA IN SEARCH OF AMICA. AFTER A WHILE

THEY FINALLY REACHED IT AND THEY THOUGHT TO GO IN, BUT MORNINGSTAR TOLD THEM THAT THEY NEED TO GO TO ATLANTIS. WITHOUT QUESTIONS THEY TURNED BACK AND WENT TO ATLANTIS. MORNINGSTAR SENT A MESSAGE TO AMICA THROUGH HIS PIGEON. AMICA RECEIVED THE MESSAGE FROM MORNINGSTAR AND SHE GAVE A BOX TO THE LEADER OF DYANAS AND SHE WENT TO ATLANTIS IN DYANAS OWN PRIVATE BOAT.

DYANA'S SHIP

SHE WAS GOING BUT THEN SHE GOT ATTACKED BY A SHIP AND SHE FELL INTO THE WATER, BUT SHE WAS LUCKY CAUSE SHE KNOWS SWIMMING AND SHE

WAS FAST AND DURABLE IN WATER. AFTER SWIMMING FOR 15KM SHE FINALLY SAW A BOAT OF MORNINGSTAR AND SAID THEM TO STOP. MORNINGSTAR TOOK HER UP ON THE BOAT. HE SAW A WOUND ON HER LEG SO HE TIED A CLOTH AND BLOCKED THE BLOOD TO COME OUT. AMICA TOLD THAT SHE SAW DANE IN THE BOAT WHICH ATTACKED HER. SHE WAS EVERY ON HIM AND WAS FILLED WITH WRATH. APEX TOLD THEM THAT THEY NEED TO GO BY SWIMMING NEAR THE ISLAND WHICH IS VERY SMALL BUT THEY NEED TO GO THERE TO HAVE A CLEAR VIEW AND BECAUSE OF THE DEPTH OF THE WATER, THEY NEED TO SWIM. MORNINGSTAR TOLD ONE OF THE MEN TO GO BUT THEN APEX TOLD "IT IS BETTER IF YOU GO 'CAUSE YOU ARE GOOD AT THIS" MORNINGSTAR SAID NO TO APEX AND SENT HIS CREWMATE TO WATCH.

THE ISLAND

CHAPTER VIII

Maledictus Navis The Cursed Ship

CAPTAIN MORNINGSTAR WAS TALKING WITH AMICA BUT THEN A MAN FROM THEIR CREW SHOUTED "ENEMIES AHEAD", ALL BECAME ALERT AND ALL TOOK THEIR GUNS AND LOADED THEIR CANNONS. DANE WAS ON ANOTHER SIDE, BUT THIS TIME MORE POWERFUL. APEX SAID TO FIRE AND "KABOOOOOM" SO MANY CANNONS FIRED AT HIS SHIP, BUT THERE WAS NOT EVEN A SINGLE CRACK OR DENT ON HIS SHIP. IT DIDN'T EVEN SHAKE. "MALEDICTUS NAVIS" THE CURSED SHIP..... AMICA TOLD SLOWLY AND IN A LOW VOICE. MORNINGSTAR SHOUTED
"TURN BACK!!! TURN BACK!!! TURN BACK I SAID!!!." THEY LUCKILY ESCAPED. APEX ASKED WHAT THIS MALEDICTUS NAVIS. AMICA TOLD "IT IS A CURSED SHIP WHICH IS ONE OF THE MOST DANGEROUS SHIPS TOO. IT CAN HOLD OVER 17 TONS OF WEIGHT AND CAN STAY STILL AND UNHARMED IN A 30 FEET HIGH TSUNAMI TOO. PEOPLE SAY, THE ONE WHO OWNS THE SHIP CAN ALSO RULE THE WORLD IN MINUTES. IT CAN BLAST 3 BROWN LOG SHIPS IN ONE FIRE. IT WAS MADE BY 3 WITCHES FOR ATLANTIS KING AND ATLANTIS KEPT IT SO CLEAN AND NEAT AND HE KEPT ALL HIS SECRETS ON HIS SHIP. MORNINGSTAR TOLD THAT HE SPARED US CAUSE IF HE WANT HE COULD KILL US AND HE ALSO TOLD THAT SOME WITCH GAVE HIM THIS SHIP. APEX ASKED WHAT TO DO THEN MORNINGSTAR TOLD "WE NEED TO GO TO THAT WITCH AND ASK HER ABOUT IT. I KNOW

THERE IS A WITCH IN THE NORTHWEST AND I AM DAMN SURE THAT SHE IS ONLY THE WITCH CAUSE SHE IS SHEIS THE BEST WITCH I HEARD OF. ALL WENT TO THE NORTHWEST AND FINALLY REACHED THE WITCHE'S HOUSE.

WITCHE'S HOUSE [IMAGINARY]

MORNINGSTAR SINGLE WENT INTO THE HOUSE AND STARTED MAKING A MESS. A WITCH CAME AND TOLD, "WHAT THE HECK ARE YOU DOING?" WHY THE HELL DID YOU GIVE MALEDICTUS TO DANE? ARE YOU MAD? YOU FUCKING WITCH, YOU ARE THE WORST WITCH HOW CAN YOU GIVE THAT STUPID DANE MALEDICTUS ARE YOU CRAZY?" WITCH GOT ANGRY SHE SAID "YOU HUMAN SCOLDED ME AND MY BROTHER LIKE DANE? I DIANA CASTS A CURSE THAT YOU WILL BE IMMORTAL BUT WILL HAVE NO HAPPINESS IN YOUR LIFE. YOU WILL FEEL 25 TIMES THE PAIN YOU FEEL FOR EVERYTHING, FOR SADNESS, FOR HURT PAIN AND ALSO IF YOU HAVE BEEN HIT WITH A SMALL BULLET YOU WILL FEEL LIKE YOU ARE DEAD" AND SHE THROWS HIM OUT OF HER HOUSE. APEX GOES INTO THE HOUSE AND DEALS CALMY WITH THE WITCH. WHICH MAKES HER CALM DOWN. HE ASKS WHY DID SHE GIVE DANE MALEDICTUS. AND SHE GIVES A REPLY "I GAVE HIM THE MALEDICTUS BECAUSE HE HELPED ME. HE MEDITATED FOR 3 MONTHS WITHOUT FOOD AND WATER AND HE PRAYED FOR ME AND WON THE MALEDICTUS."

MALEDICTUS NAVIS

CHAPTER IX

The Enquire

APEX ASKS HER TO TELL MORE CLEARLY THAN SHE REPLIES "ONE FINE DAY DANE CAME TO ME WITH BLEEDING LEGS. HE TOLD ME TO HELP HIM AND I HELPED HIM, BUT AFTER HELPING I TOLD HIM TO ASSASSINATE A KING FOR ME, BUT I DON'T KNOW THAT HE IS SO POWERFUL. HE KILLED 6 KINGS WHOM I WANTED TO BE DEAD, HE BROUGHT ME A BOOK WHICH IS PRESENT ONLY ONE ACROSS THIS WORLD AND THIS BOOK WON'T HAVE ANY COPY TOO. HE ASKED ME FOR A STRONG, DANGEROUS SHIP FOR HIM AND I GAVE HIM MALEDICTUS NAVIS. HE MEDITATED FOR MONTHS FOR THE SHIP. YOU ARE LOOKING GOOD SO I AM TELLING YOU A THING AND MAKE SURE YOU TOLD TELL ANYONE ABOUT IT. APEX TOLD OK AND ASKED

WHAT IT IS THEN SHE TOLD THAT THE OWNER OF MALEDICTUS NAVIS CAN ALSO CONTROL A SEA CREATURE CALLED KRAKEN.

KRAKEN

IT IS A GIANT SQUID THAT CAN DESTROY SHIPS EASILY. APEX GOES OUT WITH A LOT OF INFORMATION AND HE TELLS EVERYTHING TO HIS CREW. HE TOLD MORNINGSTAR TO GO TO SAVANA WITH AMICA AND BRING CODEX GIGAS AND HE TOLD THAT HE WILL GO TO THE "VALTIKI PERIOCHI" THE BIGGEST SWAMP IN THE WORLD AND HE WILL FIND A WITCH WHO CAUSES THE THE ONLY WAY TO STOP DANE IS BY CODEX GIGAS. AMICA AND MORNINGSTAR BOTH WENT TO SAVANA AND AMICA ASKED FOR A BOX FOR THE DYANA WHICH SHE GAVE A BOX EARLIER. HERE APEX WENT TOWARDS THE SWAMP AND WAS SEARCHING FOR WITCH HUTS, BUT WITCHES ARE VERY FEW AND RARE AND VALTIKI PERIOCHI IS SO HUGE THAT IT IS IMPOSSIBLE TO FIND ONE. AFTER A WHILE HE FINDS A HUT. WHEN

HE GOES IN HE SEES THAT THERE IS NO ONE INSIDE, BUT THEN A WITCH PUSHES HIM FROM BACK AND SAYS HOW DARE YOU TO ENTER MY HUT. THEN APEX SAYS "WE NEED HELP! PLEASE, I WILL GIVE YOU 500 COINS OF GOLD IF YOU AGREE WITH ME. WITCHES AGREE AND SAY "WELL WHAT IS MY WORK?" "YOU NEED TO CAST SPELLS OF CODEX GIGAS," SAYS APEX. WITCH SAYS "YOU HAVE CODEX GIGAS? HOW THE HELL DID YOU GET IT ?" NO QUESTIONS JUST YOU NEED TO DO WORK. IF YOU CAN SAY OK IF YOU CAN'T SAY NO, SAID APEX. OKAY, I AM READY TO CAST THE SPELLS OF CODEX GIGASSAYS THE WITCH. APEX ASKS HER NAME AND SHE TELLS HER NAME "MAGISSA". HERE MORNINGSTAR AND AMICA WERE ALSO SUCCESSFUL TO BRING THE CODEX GIGAS WHICH WERE IN THE BOX GIVEN TO A DYANA BY AMICA.

CODEX GIGAS PAGE [IMAGINARY]

MORNINGSTAR ASKS AMICA WHY SHE SAVED CODEX GIGAS. SHE REPLIES "CODEX GIGAS IS ONE OF THE POWERFUL WEAPONS AND IT SHOULD NOT BE IN THE WRONG HANDS. THAT'S WHY I CARRIED IT IN THE BLAST. WHEN I WAS YOUNG LIKE 16 YEARS OLD I CAME TO SAVANA AND LEARNT EVERYTHING INCLUDING OLD SCRIPTS WHICH HELPED ME NOW TO READ THE "CODEX GIGAS".

CHAPTER X

The End ?

DID YOU READ IT? WHY? ASKED MORNINGSTAR. EVERY BOOK IS GOOD IF YOU USE THOSE THINGS FOR GOOD AND I READ IT CAUSE I CAN REMEMBER EVERYTHING AND USE THOSE SPELLS FOR HUMANITY SAID AMICA. AFTER A FEW DAYS APEX AND MORNINGSTAR MEET EACH OTHER WITH THEIR WORK DONE. THEY BOTH WENT TOWARDS ATLANTIS AND THEY FOUND A WEIRD-LOOKING SHIP WHICH WAS MALEDICTUS. WHILE THEY WERE COMING MAGISSA PREPARED TO CAST HER SPELL.

MAGISSA CASTING HER SPELL [IMAGINARY]

THEY PLANNED TO DESTROY ATLANTIS AND LURE DANE TOWARDS THEM AND IN ONE SPELL KILL DANE, AND KRAKEN AND DESTROY MALEDICTUS AS WELL AS ATLANTIS. THEY BOTH WERE READY AND

MORNINGSTAR WANTS TO KILL DANE THE MOST CAUSE DANE WAS THE ONE WHO TOOK HIS EYE OFF AND MADE HIM NAKED IN FRONT OF ALL. MORNINGSTAR SAW DANE COMING SO FAST HE TOLD APEX TO START THE SPELL CASTING AND MAGISSA STARTED CASTING. DANE MADE A TO HIS CREWMATE AND THEN A GIRL WITH SO MANY WOUNDS ON HER BODY WAS TIED UP TO THEIR FLAG WHICH CAME IN APPEARANCE AFTER HIS SIGN. THE GIRL WAS CLOE. DANE KNEW THAT MORNINGSTAR IS WATCHING HIM THROUGH SPYGLASS AND FOR REAL HE WAS WATCHING. HE WAS SAD BY SEEING HIS EX-WIFE BLEEDING. HE TOLD HIS CREW TO STOP AND AS PER HIS COMMAND ALL STOPPED BUT MAGISSA WAS CASTING HER SPELL. HE CAN'T STOP HIS PLAN CAUSE IT WAS THE LIFE OF SO MANY PEOPLE. HE JUST WATCHED HIS EX-WIFE LIKE THAT. HE CAN'T DO ANYTHING EXCEPT WATCH HER. APEX WAS DONE WITH HIS WORK, BUT THEN A BIG SQUID ATTACKED ON THEIR BOAT AND THE BROWN LOG SUNK.

ALL PEOPLE CAUGHT THE PLANKS AND BARRELS AND TOOK THEIR SUPPORT. IT WAS KRAKEN. IT RAISED AMICA HIGH IN THE SKY AND TOOK HER CODEX GIGAS. AMICA FELL INTO THE WATER AFTER IT DROPPED HER OFF. DANE GOT CODEX GIGAS SO HE TOOK CLOE AND FED HER AS MEAT TO KRAKEN. MORNINGSTAR CRIED LOUDLY AND SHOUTED. THEN DANE MADE A SIGN TO KRAKEN AND KRAKEN

UNDERSTOOD THAT IT SHOULD KILL ALL THE PEOPLE WHO SURVIVED. KRAKEN WENT TOWARDS MORNINGSTAR AND STARTED FIGHTING WITH HIM. DANE GOT CODEX GIGAS AND FINALLY, HE COULD RULE THE ATLANTIS. HE WENT TO A WITCH MADE HER CAST THE SPELLS AND OWNED ATLANTIS. HE GOT SO MUCH WEALTH SO HE BOUGHT A ARMY OF 3,00,000 PEOPLE WHICH IS BIGGER THAN THE MIDLAND ARMY. HE ATTACKED MIDLAND AND OWNED IT TOO... HE ATTACKED SO MANY KINGDOMS AND OWNED OVER 21 KINGDOMS... HE OVERTOOK SAVANA AND MADE DYANAS WORK FOR THEM. HE RULED THE MAIN KINGDOMS WHICH PRODUCE MORE RESOURCES. HE BECAME SO MUCH STACKED...... NO ONE CAN KILL HIM. HE LOOTED EVERY PLACE... NO ONE CAN STOP HIM HE BECAME A DEVIL FOR ALL......

ONE OF THE 21 KINGDOMS RULED BY DANE

ENTRANCE OF ATLANTIS [IMAGINARY]

WARS DANE FOUGHT [IMAGINARY]

SAVANA AFTER DANE CAME

9 798888 051443

Printed by Libri Plureos GmbH in Hamburg, Germany